Bouki Cuts Wood

A HAITIAN FOLKTALE

retold by Amanda StJohn • illustrated by Cindy Revell

Distributed by The Child's World®
1980 Lookout Drive • Mankato, MN 56003-1705
800-599-READ • www.childsworld.com

Acknowledgments
The Child's World®: Mary Berendes, Publishing Director
The Design Lab: Kathleen Petelinsek, Design
Red Line Editorial: Editorial direction

Library of Congress Cataloging-in-Publication Data
StJohn, Amanda, 1982–
  Bouki cuts wood : a Haitian folktale / by Amanda StJohn; illustrated by
Cindy Revell.
      p. cm.
  Summary: A silly man named Bouki, believing that the old man who
passed by is a true fortune teller, asks when he will die, then behaves as if
the prediction has come true. Includes notes about Bouki tales and Haiti.
  ISBN 978-1-60973-135-9 (library reinforced : alk. paper)
  [1. Folklore–Haiti.] I. Revell, Cindy, ill. II. Title.
  PZ8.1.S8577Bou 2012
  398.2097294'02–dc23   2011010888

Printed in the United States of America in Mankato, Minnesota.
July 2011
PA02086

*onswa!* Good afternoon, my friends. I have a Bouki story for you. There are so many Bouki stories, all from the country of Haiti. But this one? This is my favorite. It is the silliest of all!

Bouki is a foolish man, and he always falls into trouble. Many people in Haiti have gone into the forest to cut trees for wood—wood to build houses, wood to make fires for cooking. When Bouki cuts wood, it is a disaster. . . .

It was a Tuesday, I am sure. An old man went for a walk down the dirt road leading to the pine forest. He wanted to cut some wood. Along the way he passed a mango tree with a goat tied to it.

Me-e-e-eh, me-e-e-eh, the goat bleated.

Where is this goat's master? he wondered. Just then, the old man heard a *chop-chop-chop.*

The old man stepped under the mango tree and looked up. There was Bouki, sitting on the end of a tree branch, chopping wood.

"*Ou byen?* Are you okay?" the old man asked Bouki.

Bouki looked around to make sure the old man was speaking to him. "*Wi.* Yes, I'm as happy as a mango, of course. Why do you ask?"

"Why? Because you are sitting on the branch that you are cutting, you fool! In a moment, the branch will break, and you will fall out of the mango tree!"

"Huh?" Bouki said, scratching his head. "Are you saying you know my future? How silly! Only a fortune-teller can tell a man his future. Be gone!"

Bouki shooed the old man away. Then, *chop-chop*, he cut the branch a little more.

There was a loud cracking noise.
Bouki's goat took three steps to the left as
the branch snapped. *Craaaack!* Bouki and
the branch fell out of the mango tree.

When Bouki could think straight again, he remembered the traveler. "My word," shouted Bouki. "That old man must be a true fortune-teller!"

At that, Bouki leaped up and ran down the dirt road after the old man. Bouki ran as fast as he could—which was not very fast.

"Old man, old man!" Bouki cried out. "Tell me, please. When am I going to die?"

"How should I know?" asked the old man. "I am just an old man."

"No," said Bouki. "You are a real fortune-teller. Just tell me when I will die."

As the old man paused to think, Bouki's goat bleated in the distance. This gave the old man a naughty idea.

"Bouki," said the old man. "You will die when your goat bleats three times!" This was not true, but the old man wanted Bouki to go away.

Bouki's face grew very pale and he whimpered. He knew that he would die very soon. His goat bleated all the time!

Bouki ran back to the mango tree as fast as he could. His goat bleated while sipping juice from a sun-warmed mango—*me-e-e-eh*.

"Shush, shush!" Bouki said, snatching away the mango.

Me-e-e-eh, the goat bleated while nibbling some grass.

Oh, no. Bouki's goat had bleated twice. Bouki was sure that if his goat bleated one more time, he would die, just as the fortune-teller had said. Bouki plucked some long grasses and wrapped them around the goat's muzzle.

"That will keep him quiet," Bouki said, folding his arms with pride.

Bouki picked up his saw. Then he climbed into the mango tree and started to cut wood the same way as before.

A new traveler came walking down the road. She saw the goat with its muzzle wrapped in long grasses. "How strange!" she exclaimed.

The traveler went to Bouki's goat and loosened the grasses. *Me-e-e-eh*, went the goat as loudly as it could. When Bouki heard this, he froze stiff on the branch he was cutting.

"That's it," Bouki said. "My goat bleated three times. That means that I am dead!" So Bouki let himself fall out of the tree as if he were dead. *Flump!*

"My word!" gasped the lady. "Bouki is dead!" She ran to the forest and gathered some men to help her carry Bouki to the bed in his little house.

"Poor Bouki," sobbed the lady.

The strong woodcutters lifted Bouki onto a hammock made of banana leaves. They began carrying him home. The nice lady untied Bouki's goat from the tree and brought it along, too.

Before long, the men arrived at the foot of a hill. There, an oak tree split the wide road into two little paths.

"Take the path on the left. Bouki lives in the wood house," said one woodcutter.

"Don't be silly!" said the other. "Bouki lives in the straw house. Go to the right."

"Actually, Bouki's house is back there," said Bouki, pointing to his own house. He kept his eyes closed, though, because he was still supposed to be dead.

"It's a ghost!" the lady screamed, looking at Bouki.

"Eeeeek!" The woodcutters shrieked like mice. They dropped poor Bouki and ran away.

Soon, no one was around except for Bouki and his goat. *Grumble, grumble.* Bouki's belly groaned with hunger.

Me-e-e-eh, me-e-e-eh, said Bouki's goat. It had found some delicious mangoes to eat. Bouki could hear his goat slurping mango juice, and it made him even hungrier.

"Hey, hey, hey!" Bouki sprang to his feet. "Save some fruit for me!"

Bouki cupped a ripe mango in his hand and took a big bite. "Goat," said Bouki, as juice dribbled down his chin, "I think I am the only dead person in the world who still loves to eat as much as when I was alive!"

Ah, that Bouki. He is so silly.

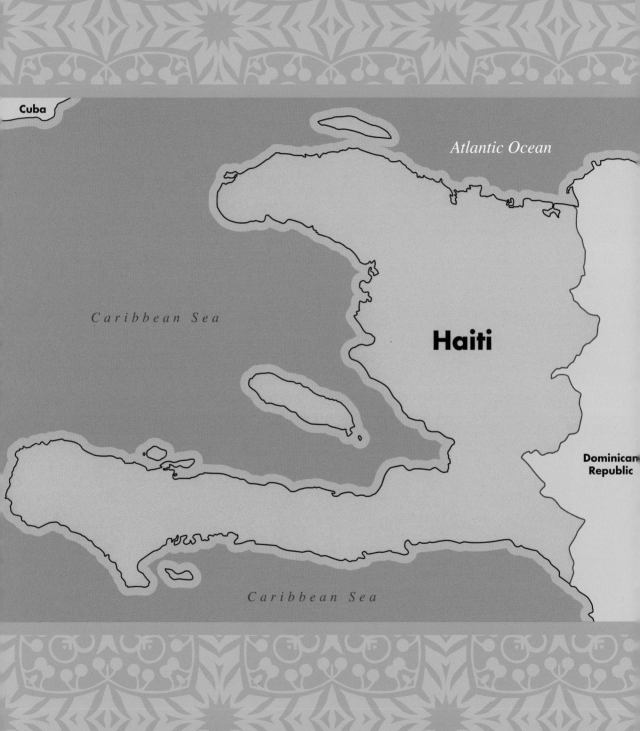

Cuba

Atlantic Ocean

Caribbean Sea

Haiti

Dominican Republic

Caribbean Sea

FOLKTALES

The people of Haiti have been telling Bouki tales for as long as anyone can remember. A *bouki* is a foolish person, or someone who is easily confused. The stories about Bouki teach us how to live and behave. Bouki makes silly mistakes so that we can learn from them. That is one important job of folktales.

A long time ago, Bouki folktales were told in Ghana, in western Africa. In those days, Bouki was a hyena who was often tricked into doing silly things by a hare. When African slaves were taken to Haiti, they brought their Bouki folktales along. But Haiti does not have hyenas, so little by little, Bouki was changed into a man.

Haiti is a tropical country. All kinds of wonderful crops grow there, including mangoes, oranges, and avocados. Pine, oak, and cedar trees grow there, too.

In the United States, we buy our things with dollars. In Haiti, people spend *gourdes*. *Gourdes* look like dollar bills, but in the old days, people actually traded real gourds. Squash, melons, and pumpkins are examples of gourds.

In Haiti, a most valuable thing for families to own is a goat. Goats can be milked. From the milk, cream, butter, cheese and soap are made. Goats like Bouki's help a person carry things across town. Goat meat itself makes a delightful dinner. A family with many goats is considered to be rich. The family can sell a goat for enough *gourdes* to send a child to school.

ABOUT THE ILLUSTRATOR

Cindy Revell lives in the Canadian countryside with her husband, a black cat, a shrimpy dog, and some chickens. She delights in using patterns and decorative elements to create whimsical and richly colored worlds for her characters. Cindy has been illustrating for over 20 years and paints in acrylics and oils. She also creates some of her art digitally.